MURDER AND RUBBER CHICKEN

WADE DALTON AND SAM CATES SHORT
STORIES BOOK 2

JIM RILEY

To the Most Beautiful

You Always Were and Always Will Be

1

"For a hundred dollars a plate, you'd think we would get something better than five-day-old rubber chicken and green beans out of a can," Wade Dalton said to his fiancée, Sam Cates.

She replied, "I'm only here because I support the addition to the Evergreen Library. It's also sorta expected as part of the job."

"You're the Sheriff, not the Librarian."

"I know, but we're supposed to mix with the public and put on a good face for the department. I would have preferred to make an anonymous donation instead."

"Me too."

"Hey kids. How are ya'll doing?" A booming voice resounded from directly behind Wade.

"Uncle Ken. What are you doing here?"

"Same as you. Except I'd rather be at Popeye's, but your aunt decided we should attend. She's afraid some of her social friends would be here and then ask her where she was if she didn't come."

"Where are you seated?"

Ken Willis pointed to the back of the room.

"As far back as they could put us. I guess my hundred dollars doesn't count as much as being the Sheriff of Evergreen County." He laughed.

"How is Aunt Marian doing?"

"Just as mean and ornery as a wild boar in rut."

"Uncle Ken, you don't mean that. She is as gentle as a lamb."

"Hah. You need to come around when I don't make it in on time to suit her. She's not a lamb at two o'clock in the morning. I can assure you of that."

Sam laughed. "I don't blame her. If you weren't our chasing girls half your age, she probably wouldn't be so upset."

He grinned. "It's when I catch one she really gets mad."

Ken strode confidently away from the table towards his wife in the rear of the hall.

Wade leaned over to Sam. "He seems like a piece of work. I've only met him once."

"Uncle Ken? He's more than a piece of work. He's tried his lines on every skirt in south Mississippi. Aunt Marian has tried to get him counseling several times, but it never works."

"Are we going to stay for the speech? We could sneak out now and go get some actual food."

"No, we can't sneak out. I have to speak to the mayor when he finishes with his speech."

"With him talking, we might be here until midnight."

"Hush, he's starting to speak. Finish your chicken."

"For what we paid, I should be eating Kobe beef."

"Shh. Act your age, little boy."

The mayor had only warmed up when a loud scream from the back of the hall interrupted him. All eyes turns toward the lady standing beside her table, looking down at the figure slumped over his plate.

"Oh my God! That's Aunt Marian!"

Sam leapt from her chair and sprinted towards her aunt. Wade followed her step for step. Reaching the table, they saw Ken Willis lifeless upper body draped over his plate. Sam checked his pulse and pulled him back in his chair. Wade could smell the faint aroma of almonds in the air.

"Cyanide, Sam. He's been poisoned."

"Okay. Everyone back away from the table. Don't touch anything. We have to preserve it for evidence."

Wade put his hand on Sam's shoulder.

"I'll take care of this if you want to be with your aunt."

She looked at him with tears in her eyes.

"Thanks."

Sam rose and escorted her aunt out of the room. Wade stood by the table ensuring nothing was disturbed until the detectives from the sheriff's office arrived. When they got to the table, Wade pointed to the people who had been seated with Ken Willis. He then went to find his fiancée and her aunt.

2

Wade looked across the desk in Sam's office.

"Any idea who put the cyanide in his food?"

She shook her long blonde hair. "No. We found traces in the glass. Somebody must have spiked the punch. It had to be the worst punch I've ever had, even at one of the city functions."

Wade grinned. "I don't know, Sam. I've had some that tasted like week old raw fish left out in the sun."

"I might prefer the raw fish."

"Any suspects?"

"Not many so far. Aunt Marian was seated right next to him. His business partner was at the same table, and one of his current girl-friends was at the table next to him. With all the mingling and whatnot, any of them could have poisoned him. Or it could have been a server, or anyone else in the room."

"Boy, I'm glad you narrowed down the suspect list to only a few hundred. I thought we'd use the telephone book instead. Then we could go in alphabetical order."

"We still can if you want. After you sort them."

Wade picked up the file and was not surprised to see cyanide poisoning listed as the cause of death. Fingerprints from the glass belonged to Ken and the server, a young lady still in her teens.

"Have you checked out the server?"

Sam nodded. "Yeah. She has no connection to Uncle Ken. She's one of the few girls in Evergreen he didn't get in the sack."

"You shouldn't talk about your dead uncle like that. It's disrespectful."

"No, what he did for years to Aunt Marian was disrespectful."

"Maybe he was only going through a mid-life crisis."

Sam laughed. "Since he was sixteen? That's an awful long crisis."

"Where do you want to start?"

"The probabilities tell us to start with the spouse. That's Aunt Marian."

3

Marian Willis lived in a blue, framed house on the edge of the city limits. The red roses in the front flower bed highlighted the crimson shudders affixed to the windows. The front porch supported two rocking chairs and a cedar swing. Sam gently knocked on the front door and was a little surprised when Marian answered.

"Aunt Marian. I didn't think you would be here by yourself."

"Yes, dear. Despite what your uncle might have told you, he was the one who was friends with everyone in town. Not me. Why don't ya'll come on in?"

They were seated in a comfortable but not posh living room. Wade noticed the furniture was of the best quality but wasn't over ornate.

"Aunt Marian, you seem to be taking Uncle Ken's death pretty well."

"Child, I'm not going to pretend our marriage wasn't over a long time ago. We stayed together in this house because it was more convenient and easier than a divorce. He didn't want to give me half of everything he owned, and I didn't want to give up his income."

"Wow. I didn't know. I'm sorry."

"Don't be sorry, Sam. I knew what Ken was when I married him. I thought I could change him, but over the years I realized he was never going to change."

"Was it to the point you wanted to harm him?"

Marian laughed out loud. "No. I didn't want to harm him. I wanted to kill him."

"Aunt Marian! Really?"

Marian shook her head. "I only said I wanted to kill him. I didn't say I killed him, although I wouldn't be too sorry if I did."

"I'm glad you didn't. I'd hate to lose my uncle and then have to arrest my aunt."

"You don't have to, Sam. I promise. I understand you two are engaged. Have you set a date yet?"

"Not yet. We're trying to pick one. Something always gets in the way."

"Life happens. We must ignore it sometimes and do what we must do."

"I agree one hundred percent." Sam shot a sideways glance at Wade, who conveniently found the ceiling very interesting. "We need to talk about Uncle Ken. Here is the list of people seated at your table. Did you know all of them?"

Sam pulled a sheet from her file and handed it to Marian. Her aunt took her time and scanned the sheet thoroughly.

"Yes, I know them."

"Did any of them have a reason to kill Uncle Ken?"

"Yes, all of them, including me."

"Did you see anyone tinkering with Uncle Ken's glass?"

"No. Is that how they poisoned him? I wondered about that."

"Yes Ma'am. Someone laced his punch with cyanide."

Marian's lips turned up in a half smile. "I'm glad whoever it is didn't get my glass mixed up with his."

"So you didn't see anyone fooling with his glass?"

"No. They served the punch first. As soon as we came in. I thought it was wine at first, but when I tasted it I realized it was grape punch."

"Were you at the table the entire time?"

"I mingled. So did everyone else at our table. You know how it is at these functions. Everyone is acting so glad to be there and seeing everyone else. The truth is only the politicians and salesmen are glad to be there, and I'm not sure about the politicians."

"His partner, Ed Gill, was seated with you. Did you hear any argument between Ed and Uncle Ken?"

"No. There couldn't have been any argument between them." Marian paused. "They weren't speaking to each other."

4

"Ed, I understand you and Ken had some differences on the business end." Wade watched the man across the expansive desk at the Real Estate offices of Gill & Willis Realty.

The tall man shook his head. "No, we didn't have some differences. We had a lot of differences."

"What were the problems?"

"Let's see. Not real big ones. Money—Clients—Marketing—Listings—Lifestyle—Honesty—Integrity—Reputation—those kinds of things. Nothing important." He said with a wry smile.

Wade chuckled. "At least you have a sense of humor about it. Some people might get upset."

Ed Gill snorted. "Get upset. I'm long past upset. But the man is dead, and we're supposed to speak well of the dead. I guess that means I can't talk about him at all."

"Can you give me some examples of the problems?"

"How many do you want?"

"One good one would give me a feel for what you're talking about. The more recent the better."

"All right. Do you know Chester Wilson?"

"Isn't he on the City Planning Commission?"

"Yep. That's the one."

Wade took out his notebook. "What specifically happened with Chester? The more specific you can be, the more helpful it will be for me to understand the dynamics."

"Dynamics. Now that is an apt word for what was going on around here."

"I take from your comment it could have turned into an explosive situation."

"Not could have. Did."

Wade nodded. "Tell me about it."

"We listed one of his rent homes he was ready to sell. He's already recouped most of his money out of it through rent. Chester has been using our firm for years and years to acquire his rent houses and dispose of them after he's got the costs back. We also manage the tenants while he owns them. So you can see his business is lucrative for us. We also manage several of the condominiums he has on the coast."

Wade scanned his notes. "The bottom line is he and his assets are a big deal to you."

"To say the least."

"What happened?"

"Chester asked us to sell one of his rent houses. Ken decided he needed to go inspect it to make sure the cleaning crew had cleaned it up, and it wasn't in a mess when we showed it to prospective buyers."

Wade furrowed his brow. "Nothing wrong with that, is there?"

"No, not at all. Chester called in and I told him we were on top of the job, and Ken was over there inspecting the house as we spoke. Chester went over and looked for himself while Ken was there."

Ed paused, and his gaze fell to his desk.

"When Chester got to the house, he didn't find Ken on top of the job."

"That doesn't sound so bad. Ken could have had other errands to run."

"No, instead of finding him on top of the job, he found him on top of his seventeen-year-old daughter."

Wade chuckled. "I can see where that might sour a relationship with your best client."

"Yeah, a little more than sour it. Chester wanted to kill him. He threatened to have him arrested, but his daughter talked him out of it."

"Was Chester at the Library Expansion fundraiser? I don't remember seeing him there."

"He was there for a few minutes. I talked to him and apologized for the umpteenth time. I still have him as a client."

"Does the company now belong to you? What happens to Ken's share?"

"We had a rights-of-survivorship agreement meaning I can buy his share of the company from his estate at fair market value."

"What is the fair market value of the company?"

Ed ran his hand through his hair.

"It will be determined by an independent appraiser, but the value should come out somewhere around twelve million for the entire company. I will pay the estate half of the value so I'm looking for a payout to Marian of about six million."

"Wow. Marian will receive six million dollars because Ken is dead?"

"That's how we worked it out. My wife would have received the same amount if I had died."

"Nice. Will she be required to do anything with the company? Will she be expected to come to work?"

"Nope. Once I buy her out, she and the estate will no ties to my real estate company."

"So she can take the six mil and go have fun at the mall or the luxury car dealership or wherever she wants?"

"Not bad, huh?"

"Not at all. I didn't know killing Ken could be so lucrative."

Ed laid his hand on his desk. "Are you saying you think Marian poisoned Ken?"

Wade shook his head. "Not at all. She is one of several people who had a motive and the opportunity. Others would include you and Chester and I've only begun the investigation."

"A part of me wishes I had killed him, but I didn't, Wade. I have no idea who did. I'd buy them a drink and hire them the best lawyer in town if I knew who did it."

"Sam and I hope to help you find out."

5

"What is it, Sam? You look like you've seen a ghost."

Sam handed the piece of paper she had been reading over her desk to Wade. On the paper were block letters cut out of a newspaper. The letters read 'How does it feel to lose a relative? More to come.' Wade read the note again to make sure he was interpreting it correctly.

"This was addressed to you?"

Sam nodded. "Yes."

"Wow."

Sam laughed nervously, "I couldn't have said it any better myself."

Wade leaned back in his chair.

"This means we've been going down the wrong trail. We need to be looking for someone who wants revenge on you and not someone mad at Ken. His only fault was being your uncle."

Sam's eyes widened as the realization sunk in.

"Yes, somebody wants to get back at me for something, and I don't have a clue what that might be."

"Who have you pissed off lately?"

"Other than you?"

"Yeah, I get mad at you, but I'm not gonna kill someone over it. Must've been one of your other boyfriends."

"I don't need any more headaches. You're enough of one."

"So who else is there?"

"That's the problem. I don't know anyone that upset with me to kill Uncle Ken. And now they're saying they're getting ready to kill someone else close to me."

"I guess we need to start on your files and see if anything pops out."

Sam groaned. "There has to be a better way. Do you realize how many files we have around here?"

"We don't have to go through all of them. Just the ones where somebody died. The note said you need to know how it feels to lose someone. I assume it meant someone close to them is no longer living because of you."

"Or it could mean whoever it is may be in prison for the rest of their lives."

"Let's start with the deaths and then progress to the life sentences. At least we'll think we have a plan."

Sam called her deputies into her office and showed them the letter she received. After each of them had read it, she divided up the case file numbers for the last two years.

"We're looking for someone that either died or has been incarcerated for a long time. We also think the relatives think the circumstances were the fault of our office. If you find anything at all resembling what we're looking for, mark it and send the file to my computer. Wade and I will go through all of them you send."

One deputy stepped forward.

"Sam, this could take all night and most of the morning."

"I know, Jeremy. But I don't see where we have any choice. Someone else will die if we don't find out who sent this note."

"Yes, Ma'am. Are you authorizing the overtime pay?"

"Definitely. If we can save a life, it will be worth it."

"No problem, Sam. I just wanted to make sure before I call my wife."

"Tell her not to wait up, Jeremy. We may get through in time for you to have brunch with her tomorrow."

"Okay, Sam. At least she'll be happy with the overtime pay. We'll be able to pay an extra bill or two."

"Get after it. I don't know how much time we have."

Minutes turned into hours. Every deputy was seated at a computer, carefully scanning files from the previous twenty-four months. Each file of interest was sent to Wade. He then sent the ones he deemed appropriate to Sam. She reviewed each of those with great scrutiny. The deputies voted for Chinese food for dinner. The receptionist ordered family sized portions of Moo Goo Gai Pan, Kung Pao Chicken, Shrimp with Lobster Sauce and Twice Cooked Pork. She added egg rolls and pork fried rice along with a couple of orders of steamed dumplings. None of it was left by midnight.

Only three files emerged to the top of the list by the early morning hours.

"These are the most promising ones as far as I can tell." Sam said in the middle of a yawn.

Wade read the names on the files out loud. "Raymond, Stringer, and Clinton. I'm familiar with the Raymond shooting and the Stringer affair. Tell me again about the Clinton case. I know I read it sometime last night, but I can't remember the details about that one."

Sam looked at the ceiling. "One of my deputies spotted a car weaving on Highway 11 just north of Picayune. He hit his lights and fell in behind it. Earl Clinton was driving the car. He was only seventeen. When the car didn't pull over, he turned on his siren. The car refused to stop and sped away. The deputy gave chase and radioed for backup. Two other deputies set up a roadblock just this side of Carriere. When Earl saw the roadblock, he gunned the engine and rammed into the patrol cars. He was killed instantly. Fortunately, none of our deputies were injured."

"Was he under the influence?"

"No. That's the sad part of the story. Earl was a diabetic and didn't take his meds. There's no telling what he was seeing or thought he was seeing."

"I'm guessing the Clintons blamed you and your officers for his death."

"Yeah. They filed a lawsuit, but the judge tossed it out of court. The officers followed standard protocol and Earl was an immediate danger to other drivers. There wasn't much else we could have done."

"I still understand the parents' grief. A parent should never have to bury one of their kids."

Sam swept her hand through her long blonde hair. "I couldn't agree with you more but I still don't know what we could have done differently."

"Oh, I'm not blaming the department or your deputies. It's just a tragic case."

Sam sighed. "That's why it's at the top of the list. I need to let the staff go home. These guys are worn out and the morning crew should be here in a few minutes."

"Okay, I want to scan these three files and see if I can come up with something."

Wade wearily rose and plodded to the kitchenette to retrieve a cup of coffee. Wanda exited the area with a bright smile.

"Good morning, Wade. I trust you had a wonderful night."

"No. But I hope it was a productive one."

"Well, go back to the office. I'll bring you some coffee. You like it black, don't you?"

"Yes, thank you."

"Oh, and I brought some doughnuts in. Do you still like the chocolate with sprinkles?"

"You don't forget, do you Wanda?"

She beamed. "I try not to. And tell Sam I'll bring her some bran doughnuts when she gets back."

"Thanks, Wanda."

Wade shuffled back to Sam's office and plopped down in the chair opposite Sam's. His eyelids were struggling to stay open when he smelled the invigorating aroma of the coffee.

"Thanks, again."

"It's a pleasure to serve you, Wade."

Somewhere in the deep recesses of Wade's mind, bells clanged and lights danced. However, the cause of the disturbance remained buried behind the wall of fatigue. Sam re-entered her office and stopped.

"Uh oh. What's wrong?"

Wade looked at her unknowingly.

"What do you mean?"

"You're sitting there with three chocolate doughnuts with sprinkles on the table in front of you and you haven't touched them. Something is badly wrong in the worst way."

Wade tried to laugh. "That's why you're the sheriff. You're observant."

"No, I know you and I know you can't resist chocolate doughnuts no matter how tired you are."

Wade was still trying to clear the fog from his head. He took a long sip of coffee before answering Sam.

"It was something that Wanda said. I can't figure out what it was she said or why it struck a nerve, but it did."

Sam chuckled. "Have a little more caffeine. It'll come to you. In fact, I could use some myself." She stuck her arm across the desk and grabbed a chocolate doughnut.

"Wow. It has been a long night if you've resorted to eating the same things I do."

Sam's phone rang on her desk. She picked it up and listened only for a few seconds before slamming the receiver back down. She leapt from her chair.

"C'mon. Aunt Marian's house is on fire!"

6

"Definitely arson. No doubt about it, Sam." The fire inspector poked through the rubble left of Marian Willis's home. "See the dark stain here. That's the origin of the fire. If you stick your nose down close to it, you'll smell the accelerant. Probably gasoline, if I had to guess."

"How long ago was it set?"

"Let's see. We got here about an hour ago. From the looks of things when we got here, it was probably burning fifteen or twenty minutes by then. No one was home, and the neighbors didn't notice it for a while."

"How long will your investigation take?"

"We should be through by noon tomorrow. I'll be able to get you a report before quitting time if you need it."

"Yeah. I think this may be part of something bigger. As soon as you get it to me, I'd appreciate it."

"Any clues who might have set it?"

"Not yet. We found an old gas can in the shed, but I don't think it was used for the accelerant for this fire. We can't be sure."

Sam noticed Marian standing by her car on the street.

"Aunt Marian, I'm so sorry this happened. Are you okay?"

"Yes, child. I'm fine. That old house didn't mean anything to me. That was Ken's house. He loved it more than he loved me sometimes."

Sam put her arms around her aunt.

"I'm afraid you and Uncle Ken got caught up in someone's vendetta against me and the department."

"Who?"

"We don't know yet. We spent all of last night and most of the morning going through our files to figure it out. But we haven't had a lot of success yet."

"Don't worry about the house, Sam. We had insurance on it and I had nothing in there I can't live without. At least no one got hurt or killed. That's the most important thing right now."

"Where will you go, Aunt Marian?"

"We've got a beach house. I think I'll go there and spend my afternoons watching the tide come in."

"Are you sure you've okay?"

"Yes. I'm fine. Don't worry about me. Go after whoever is sending you those notes. I know how to take care of myself."

"Do you want a deputy to follow you to the beach house?"

"No, No. Sam, I've been independent ever since I married your uncle. He's never really been there for support. I know how to take care of myself. Don't worry."

7

"Hey, Sleepyhead. I brought you some more doughnuts. Chocolate with sprinkles just like you like them." Sam said to Wade after she entered the Sheriff's office.

Wade rubbed his stomach. "All of my fat cells are clapping right now." He said with a big grin.

Sam shook her head. "Yeah, but your brain cells are saying 'No, No. We don't want to go into another sugar coma'."

"But they're smiling when they say it. All of that sugar hitting them at one time. They'll think they're on vacation."

"Which they will be with the overload. Hold on, and I'll put them in the microwave for you. Thirteen seconds and they'll taste just like coming out of the grease."

"You're the best, Sam."

"Anything I can do to be of service."

"That's it, Sam. Why didn't I think of it before?"

"What's it?"

Wade didn't answer, but grabbed the extensive file from Sam's desk. He shuffled through the pages, scanning each one for the key data. When he reached the end, he shook his head and started over from the first page, going more carefully through each page. About three quarters through the file for the second time, he stopped and stared at the page.

He looked up at Sam. "Do you have a list of the people who were interviewed at the Library fundraiser?"

Sam reached under a pile of papers on her desk and pulled out a manila folder.

"Right here. What are you looking for?"

"When you said 'serve', a bell went off. Do you know who the server was at Ken's table?"

"Sheila Broussard is her name. We interviewed her, and she didn't know any of the people at the fundraiser. She's only nineteen, I believe."

"Married, right?"

"Uh. Hold on. Let me look."

Sam pulled out another paper showing a background check for Sheila Broussard.

"She married this year."

Wade smiled. "And her maiden name was?"

"Clinton. Sheila Clinton. Oh my God! She's Earl Clinton's sister."

"That's what I was trying to get out of the fog. I guess the extra sugar from the doughnuts this morning helped."

"We've got to go talk to Mrs. Sheila."

8

"Sheila, thanks for talking to us on short notice."

Sheila Broussard lived in a double-wide mobile home in one of the few trailer parks in town that the owner kept mowed and in order. The home was spacious but plain. Wade and Sam sat on the modest sofa and Sheila sat on a bar stool at the counter.

"What can I do for you? I answered all the questions your deputies had right after the function."

"We only have a couple of more, Sheila."

"Okay, but I have to go to work in a few minutes. The owner gets mad when we don't show up on time for our shift, and I have the lunch shift today."

"No problem. We won't be long. If you get there a few minutes late, have April call us and we'll explain. We've known April since before she became the owner. She won't mind in a situation like this."

"It's not only that. I need the hours. My husband is out of work and I don't make much down at the restaurant, so I need to get in as many hours as possible."

"Tell us about the Library Expansion event. How were you selected to work at it?"

"I've worked a lot of the events at the hotel. Whenever I can, I fill in when they have a big to-do happening if it doesn't conflict with my work schedule. April has let me swap shifts a couple of time with the other waitresses at the Evergreen Restaurant. She knows Jim, that's my husband; she knows he's out of work and she's been flexible if I'm able to work at the hotel and earn some extra money."

"This wasn't the first event you've worked at the hotel. Is that correct?"

"Yeah. I've work dozens of them. We don't get tips when we work there, but the straight pay is better."

Sam leaned forward on the sofa. "Who selected you to work that section of the room?"

"I volunteered for it."

"Why did you want that section?"

Sheila glanced at Wade but turned back to Sam. "Please don't tell them."

"Tell them what, Sheila?"

"I can't go for three hours without a smoke. I know it's a nasty habit, but I can't break it. I always try to get the back section so I can get a cigarette. I really don't take long, just a minute or two. Do you have to tell them?"

"No. We're trying to get some background on the event and you were the server for Uncle Ken's table."

"Uncle Ken? I didn't know he was your uncle. The deputies didn't mention it when I talked to them."

"Are you sure you didn't know, Sheila?"

Sheila had a puzzled expression on her face.

"How would I know something like that? I didn't know you or him before all of this happened."

"Okay. Why didn't you tell the deputies your brother was Earl Clinton?"

Sheila's expression clouded over. "Why? What difference does that make?"

"You are his sister. Correct?"

"Yes, I was. He's dead."

Sam nodded. "I know. Your parents sued our department because of his death."

"Oh, yeah. I had forgotten about that. It's been so long ago. Still, what does that have to do with the man's death at the function?"

"We're trying to find out. Do your parents still hold a grudge against the Sheriff's department?"

Sheila nodded. "They probably always will. They shouldn't have had to bury Earl. It almost killed them."

Sam leaned ever more forward. "I'm sorry, Sheila. I don't want to rehash the case today, but there really wasn't anything else we could do differently. We did everything properly and by the book in the incident."

"You've got to understand it from their perspective. He was their oldest and he was Mom's favorite. When he died, a large part of their lives died with him. They had to blame someone for his death. They couldn't accept it was Earl's fault."

"How about you, Sheila? Do you blame the Sheriff's department?"

Sheila didn't answer for several seconds. When she did, she looked Sam straight in her eyes.

"Some. Ya'll didn't have to chase Earl into the roadblock. But I knew Earl and what he was doing better than my parents. It was only a matter of time before he got into trouble. I didn't know the trouble was going to kill him."

A tear dropped from her cheek.

"Did you blame any person at the Sheriff's office?"

"I don't know any of the people who work there. What happened to Earl was tragic. I wish it had never happened. But it did and I have to go on living my life. I can't stay angry if I want to go on. I'm more concerned with how me and my husband are going to pay next month's rent than anything else. Do you have many more questions? I need to get to work."

"We'll call you if we think of anything else."

"Can I ask you a favor?"

Sam nodded. "Sure. What do you need?"

"Could you write a quick note to April explaining why I'm late for work?"

Sam nodded. She took out one of her business cards and jotted a quick note on the back and handed the card to Sheila.

"Here. This should do it."

9

Back in the patrol car, Wade laughed.

"I don't think I've seen anyone ask for an excuse note since high school."

Sam smiled. "She's not that long out of school. She's only nineteen. I bet April can be tough on the waitresses at the restaurant. She's probably had a tough time making sure they show up on time for work."

Wade shook his head. "Yeah, but a note?"

Sam's eyes suddenly widened. A huge grin spread across her face.

"I've got it, Wade. I know who killed Uncle Ken."

Wade stared blankly at her across the seat. She glanced over at him.

"Don't look at me like that. I know. I don't have any proof, but I know."

"Can we get proof?"

"I don't see how, Wade."

"Tell me what you know, and we'll put a plan together."

10

"What a view?" Sam looked out the beach house window over the Gulf of Mexico. The waves, rolling in on the beach, white-capped about a hundred yards offshore. Seagulls swooped down, picking up any scraps of food left by the tourists.

"This is one reason I wasn't too upset over losing the other house. I like this one better and I can use the insurance off of the other one to take a cruise or two."

"From what I understand the bank is worth, I don't think the cost of a cruise will be a big obstacle, Aunt Marian."

"Hopefully, it won't take long to settle the estate."

Sam smiled at her aunt. "The only problem is you won't be able to accept your portion of the estate."

Marian jerked her head up. "Huh?"

Sam looked directly at her.

"When you killed Uncle Ken, you forfeited any share of the estate."

"But I didn't kill him, Sam. Why would I?"

"I don't know exactly why. You might have tired of his running around or his lack of respect for you. I only know you poisoned him at the Library function."

"That sounds like a wonderful theory, Sam. But here in the good old USA, you need proof and you don't have any."

"Not true, Aunt Marian. I have your own words to prove it. You were the only one who had the means, the motive and the opportunity."

"Humph! All of that is circumstantial, dear."

"Your words aren't."

"What words?"

Sam glanced at Wade before continuing. "You told me in front of the burning house to go after whoever sent the note. Nobody outside of my office knew about the note. I'd only told you someone was out to get me. I never mentioned the note to you or anyone else."

Marian stammered. "I — uh — I must have heard it from one of your deputies."

"No, Aunt Marian. I was the only one there from our office and I didn't tell you."

"That's not proof of murder, Sam."

"No, but this is. It's the receipt for the cyanide. We found where it was bought."

"That's not possible. The maid bought it and paid cash. You couldn't have traced it to me."

Sam leaned back and relaxed. "We didn't, Aunt Marian. This is a blank piece of paper."

NOTES

Murder and Rubber Chicken is a short story the Wade Dalton and Sam Cates series. It features the dynamic duo with even greater challenges.

I have taken great literary license with the geography and data of south Mississippi. They are wonderful and a great way to experience the deep South culture. I lived there for over five years and found it to be one of the most desirable places on earth if you enjoy the outdoors, great cuisine and remarkable people.

There are so many people to thank:

My family, Linda, Josh, Dalton & Jade

David and Sara Sue

C D and Debbie Smith

My brother and sister-in-law, Bill & Pam

My sister, Debbie

My sister-in-law and her husband, Brenda & Jerry

The Sunday School class at Zoar Baptists

Any and all mistakes, typos and errors are my fault and mine alone. If you would like to get in touch with me, go to my web site at http:// jimrileyweb.wix.com/jimrileybooks.

I thank you for reading ***Murder and Rubber Chicken*** and hope you will also enjoy the rest my books.

Dear reader,

We hope you enjoyed reading *Murder and Rubber Chicken*. Please take a moment to leave a review, even if it's a short one. Your opinion is important to us.

Discover more books by Jim Riley at

https://www.nextchapter.pub/authors/jim-riley

Want to know when one of our books is free or discounted? Join the newsletter at

http://eepurl.com/bqqB3H

Best regards,

Jim Riley and the Next Chapter Team

Lightning Source UK Ltd.
Milton Keynes UK
UKHW041828040321
379813UK00008B/501/J